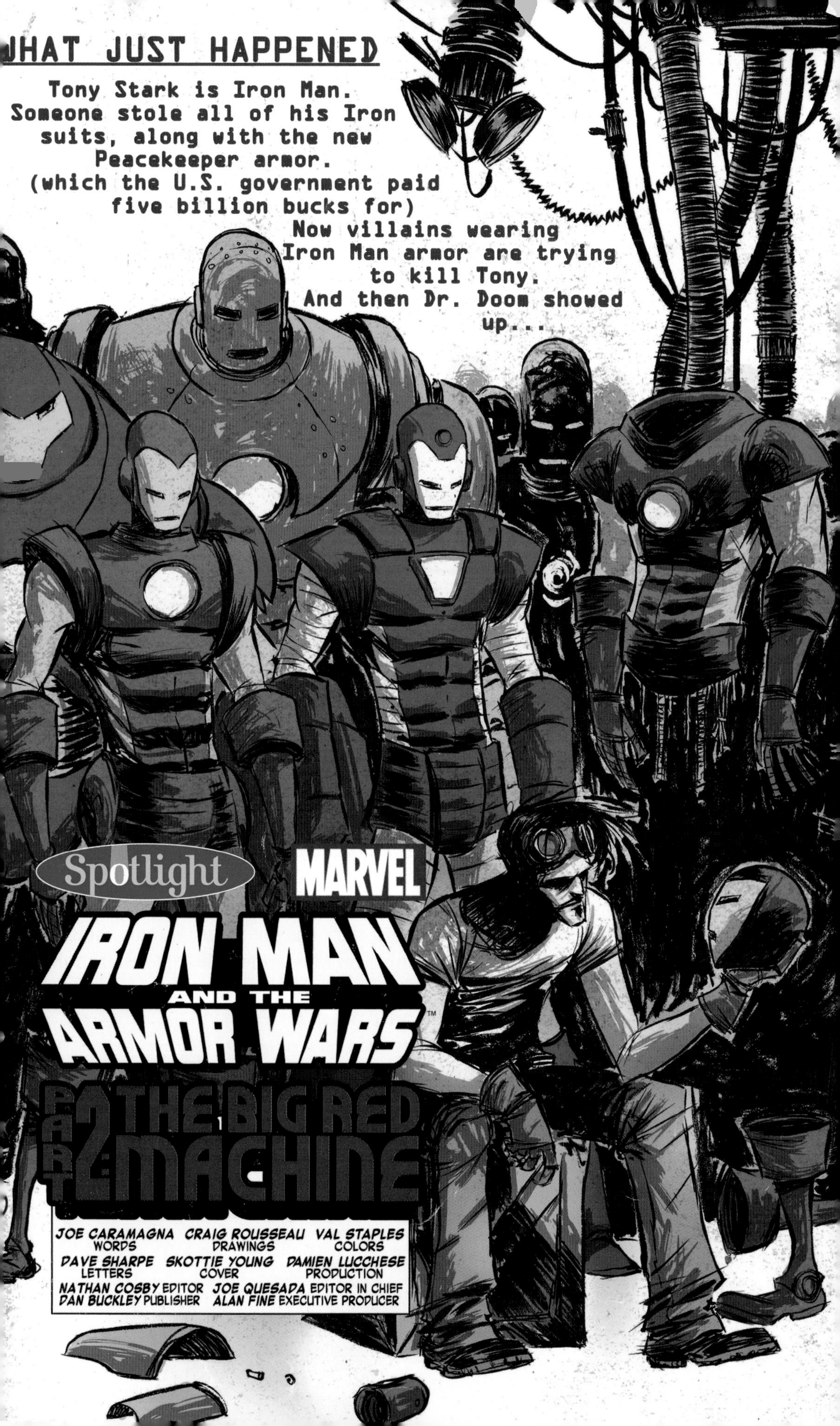
WHAT JUST HAPPENED
Tony Stark is Iron Man. Someone stole all of his Iron suits, along with the new Peacekeeper armor. (which the U.S. government paid five billion bucks for)
Now villains wearing Iron Man armor are trying to kill Tony. And then Dr. Doom showed up...
Spotlight
MARVEL
IRON MAN AND THE ARMOR WARS™
PART 2: THE BIG RED MACHINE
JOE CARAMAGNA WORDS
CRAIG ROUSSEAU DRAWINGS
VAL STAPLES COLORS
DAVE SHARPE LETTERS
SKOTTIE YOUNG COVER
DAMIEN LUCCHESE PRODUCTION
NATHAN COSBY EDITOR
JOE QUESADA EDITOR IN CHIEF
DAN BUCKLEY PUBLISHER
ALAN FINE EXECUTIVE PRODUCER

Visit us at www.abdopublishing.com

Reinforced library bound editions published in 2014 by Spotlight, a division of the ABDO Group, PO Box 398166, Minneapolis, MN 55439. Spotlight produces high-quality reinforced library bound editions for schools and libraries. Published by agreement with Marvel Characters, Inc.

Printed in the United States of America, Melrose Park, Illinois.
042013
012014
♻ This book contains at least 10% recycled material.

marvel.com
© 2013 Marvel

Library of Congress Cataloging-in-Publication Data

Caramagna, Joe.
  Iron Man and the armor wars / story by Joe Caramagna ; art by Craig Rousseau. -- Reinforced library edition.
       volumes cm
  Summary: "Cash, cars, boats, houses...Tony Stark has got it all. The only thing that could ruin his day? If every single one of his Iron Man armors were stolen, and then turned against him"-- Provided by publisher.
  ISBN 978-1-61479-164-5 (part 1: Down and out in Beverly Hills) --
  ISBN 978-1-61479-165-2 (part 2: The big red machine) --
  ISBN 978-1-61479-166-9 (part 3: How I learned to love the bomb) --
  ISBN 978-1-61479-167-6 (part 4: The Golden Avenger strikes back)
  1. Graphic novels. I. Rousseau, Craig, illustrator. II. Title.
  PZ7.7.C3653Iro 2013
  741.5'3--dc23
                        2013003434

All Spotlight books are reinforced library bindings
and manufactured in the United States of America.

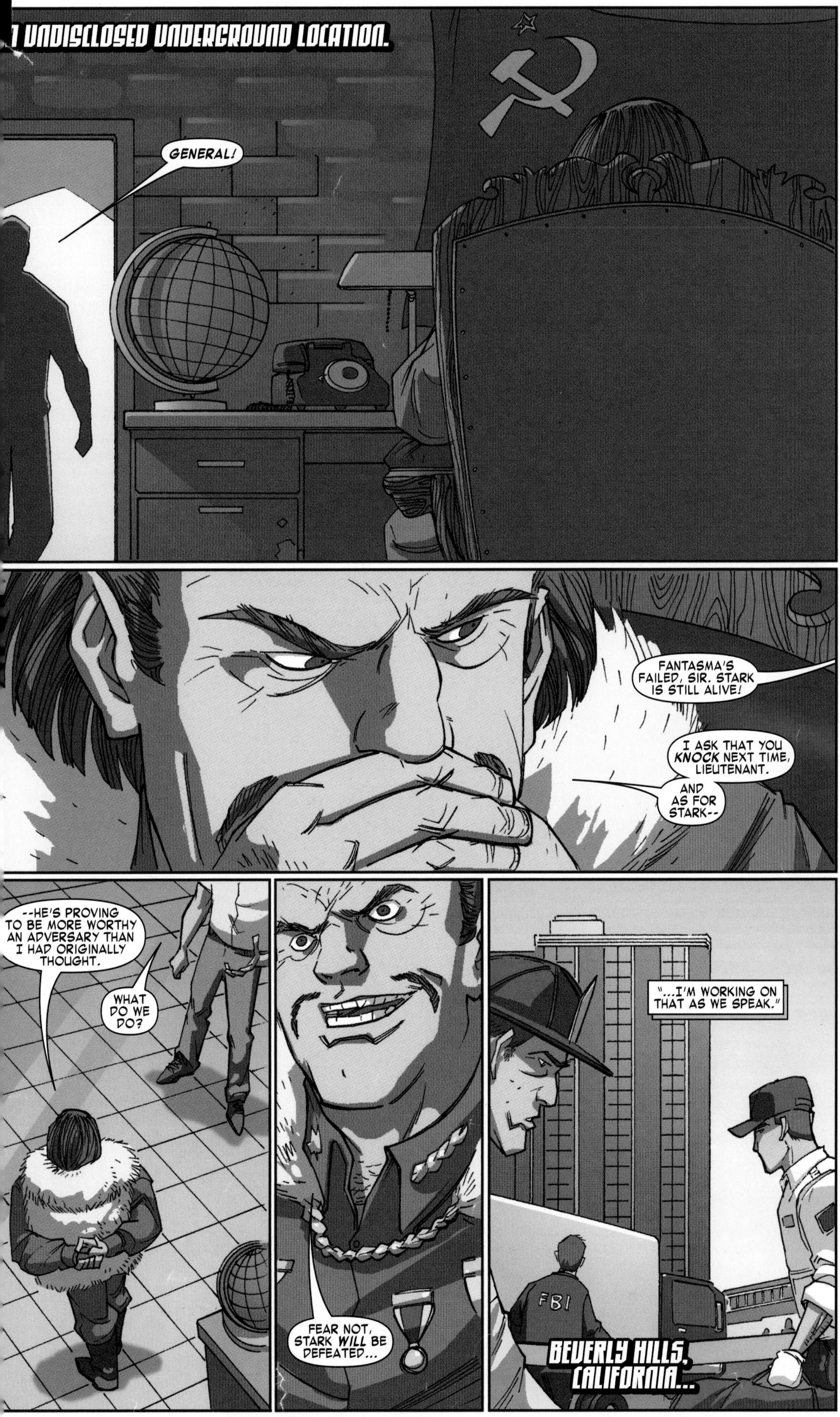
N UNDISCLOSED UNDERGROUND LOCATION.
GENERAL!
FANTASMA'S FAILED, SIR. STARK IS STILL ALIVE!
I ASK THAT YOU KNOCK NEXT TIME, LIEUTENANT.
AND AS FOR STARK--
--HE'S PROVING TO BE MORE WORTHY AN ADVERSARY THAN I HAD ORIGINALLY THOUGHT.
WHAT DO WE DO?
FEAR NOT, STARK WILL BE DEFEATED...
"...I'M WORKING ON THAT AS WE SPEAK."
FBI
BEVERLY HILLS, CALIFORNIA...

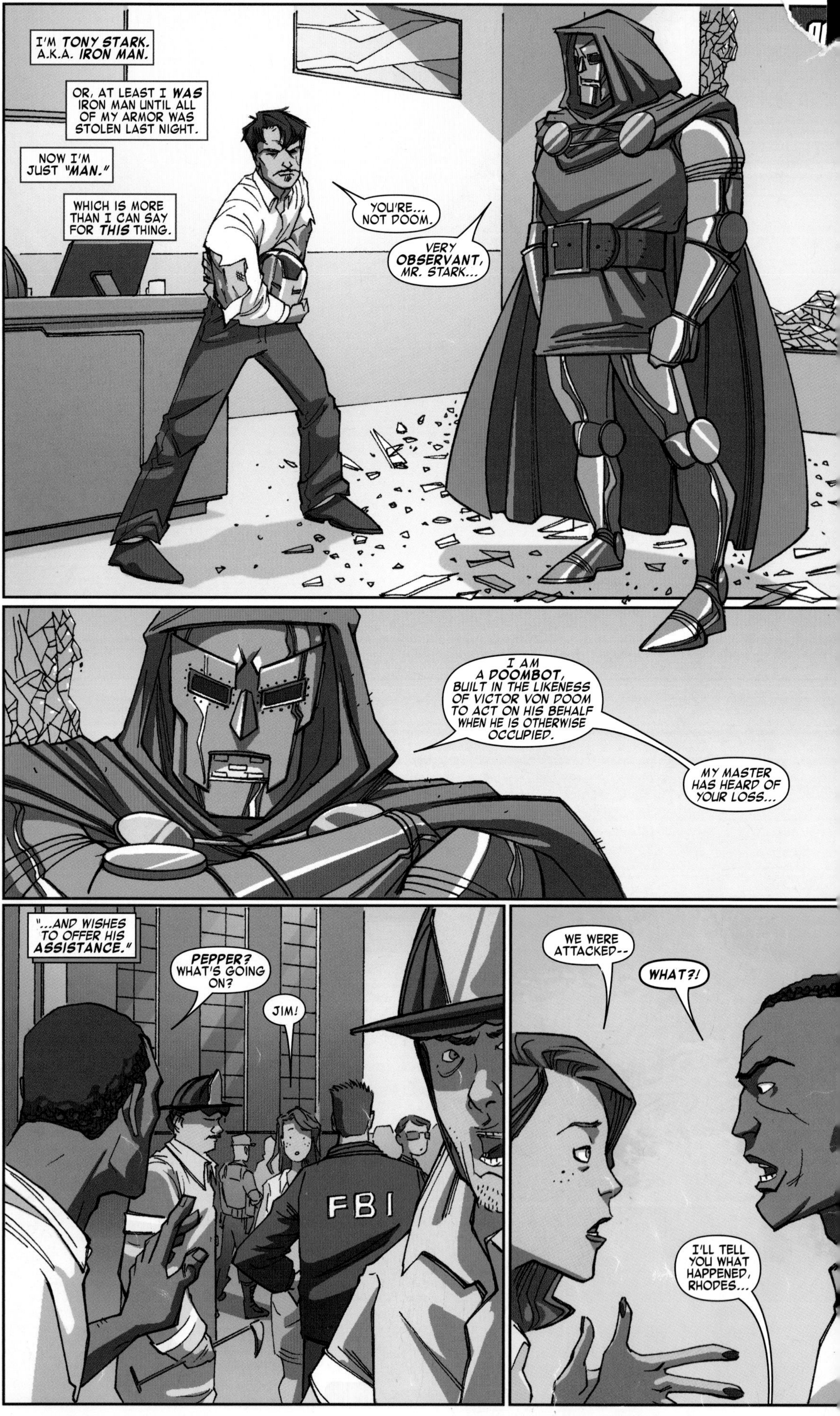
I'M TONY STARK. A.K.A. IRON MAN.
OR, AT LEAST I WAS IRON MAN UNTIL ALL OF MY ARMOR WAS STOLEN LAST NIGHT.
NOW I'M JUST "MAN."
WHICH IS MORE THAN I CAN SAY FOR THIS THING.
YOU'RE... NOT DOOM.
VERY OBSERVANT, MR. STARK...
I AM A DOOMBOT, BUILT IN THE LIKENESS OF VICTOR VON DOOM TO ACT ON HIS BEHALF WHEN HE IS OTHERWISE OCCUPIED.
MY MASTER HAS HEARD OF YOUR LOSS...
"...AND WISHES TO OFFER HIS ASSISTANCE."
PEPPER? WHAT'S GOING ON?
JIM!
FBI
WE WERE ATTACKED--
WHAT?!
I'LL TELL YOU WHAT HAPPENED, RHODES...

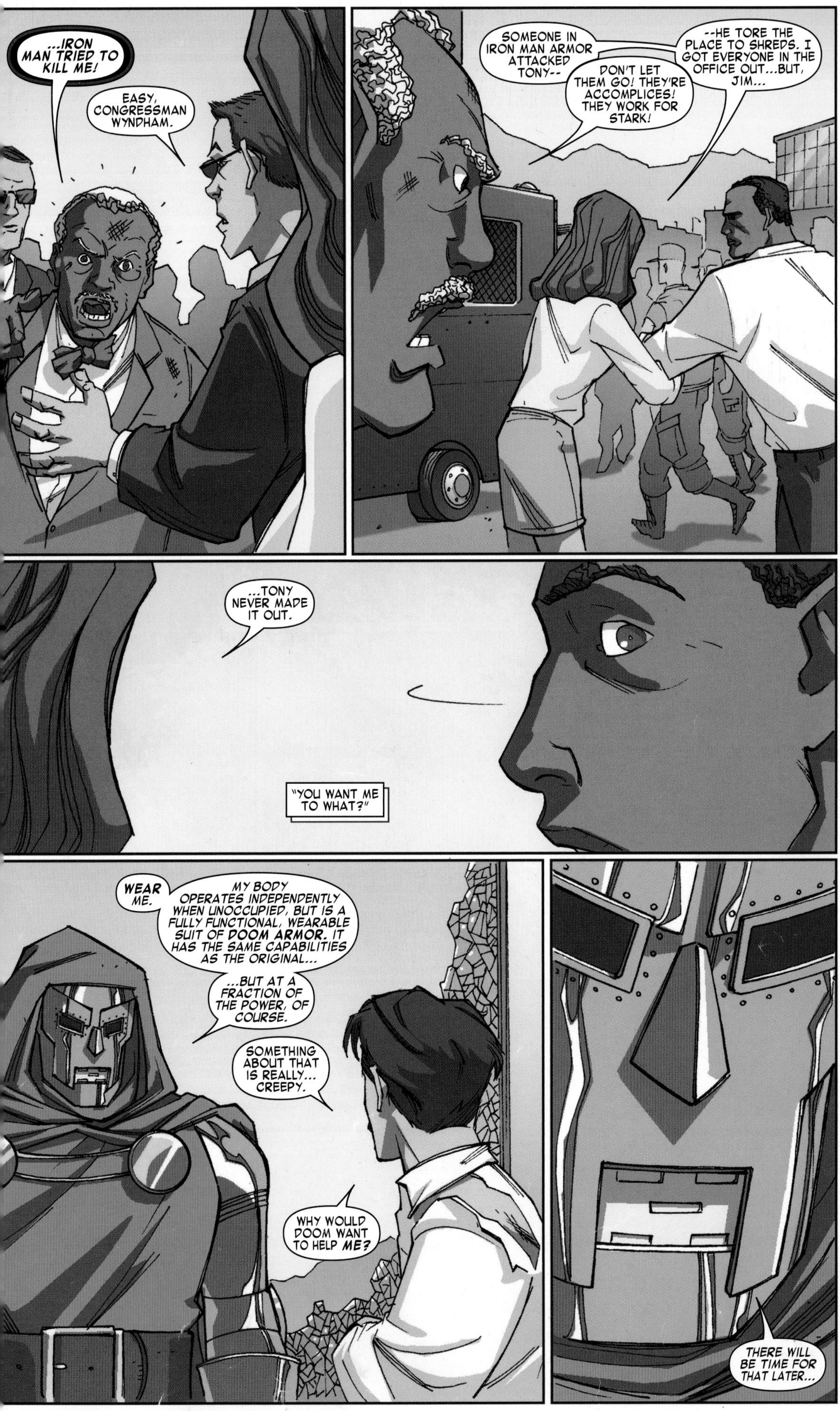
...IRON MAN TRIED TO KILL ME!
EASY, CONGRESSMAN WYNDHAM.
SOMEONE IN IRON MAN ARMOR ATTACKED TONY--
--HE TORE THE PLACE TO SHREDS. I GOT EVERYONE IN THE OFFICE OUT...BUT, JIM...
DON'T LET THEM GO! THEY'RE ACCOMPLICES! THEY WORK FOR STARK!
...TONY NEVER MADE IT OUT.
"YOU WANT ME TO WHAT?"
WEAR ME.
MY BODY OPERATES INDEPENDENTLY WHEN UNOCCUPIED, BUT IS A FULLY FUNCTIONAL, WEARABLE SUIT OF DOOM ARMOR. IT HAS THE SAME CAPABILITIES AS THE ORIGINAL...
...BUT AT A FRACTION OF THE POWER, OF COURSE.
SOMETHING ABOUT THAT IS REALLY... CREEPY.
WHY WOULD DOOM WANT TO HELP ME?
THERE WILL BE TIME FOR THAT LATER...

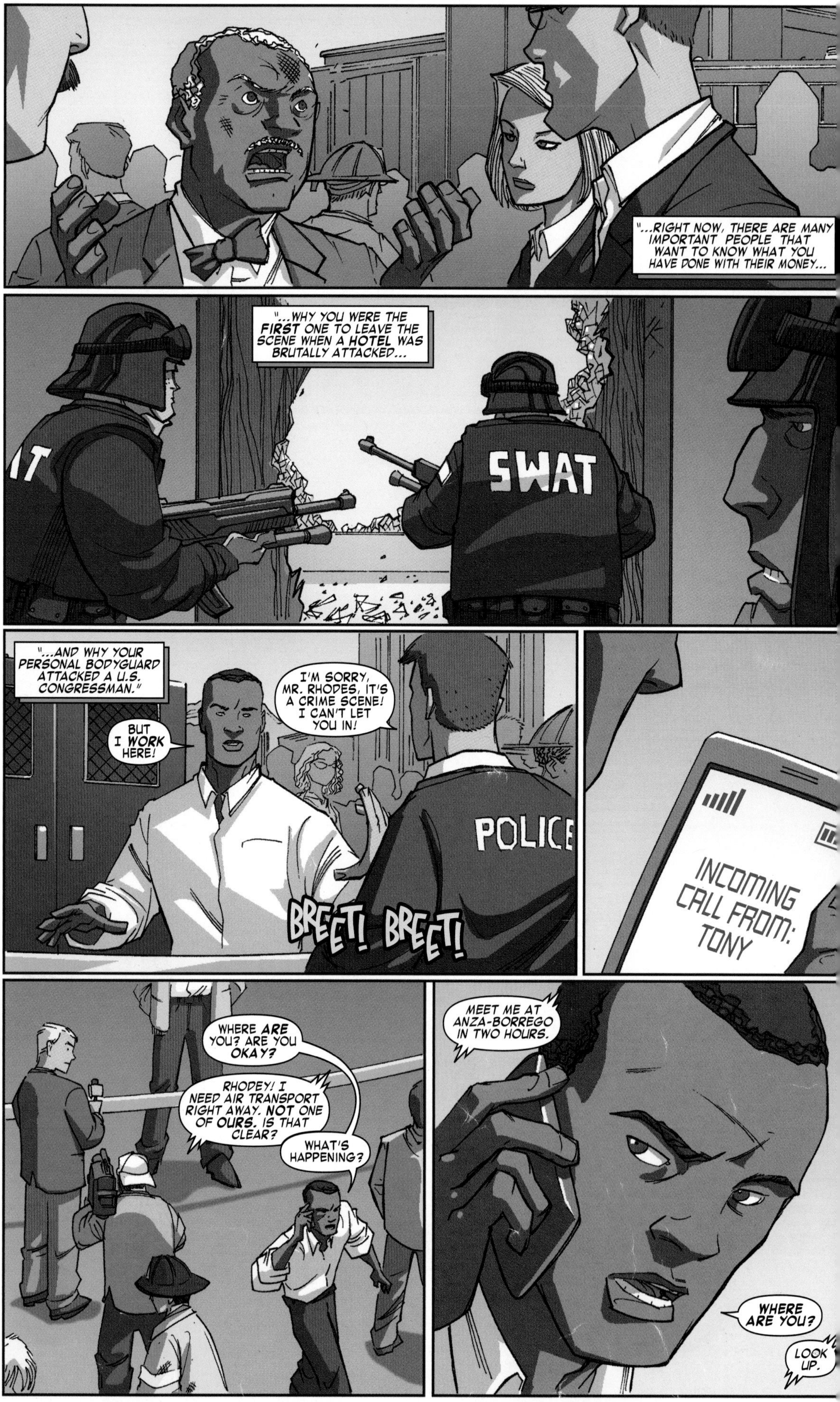
"...RIGHT NOW, THERE ARE MANY IMPORTANT PEOPLE THAT WANT TO KNOW WHAT YOU HAVE DONE WITH THEIR MONEY...
"...WHY YOU WERE THE FIRST ONE TO LEAVE THE SCENE WHEN A HOTEL WAS BRUTALLY ATTACKED...
SWAT
"...AND WHY YOUR PERSONAL BODYGUARD ATTACKED A U.S. CONGRESSMAN."
I'M SORRY, MR. RHODES, IT'S A CRIME SCENE! I CAN'T LET YOU IN!
BUT I WORK HERE!
POLICE
BREET! BREET!
INCOMING CALL FROM: TONY
WHERE ARE YOU? ARE YOU OKAY?
RHODEY! I NEED AIR TRANSPORT RIGHT AWAY. NOT ONE OF OURS. IS THAT CLEAR?
WHAT'S HAPPENING?
MEET ME AT ANZA-BORREGO IN TWO HOURS.
WHERE ARE YOU?
LOOK UP.

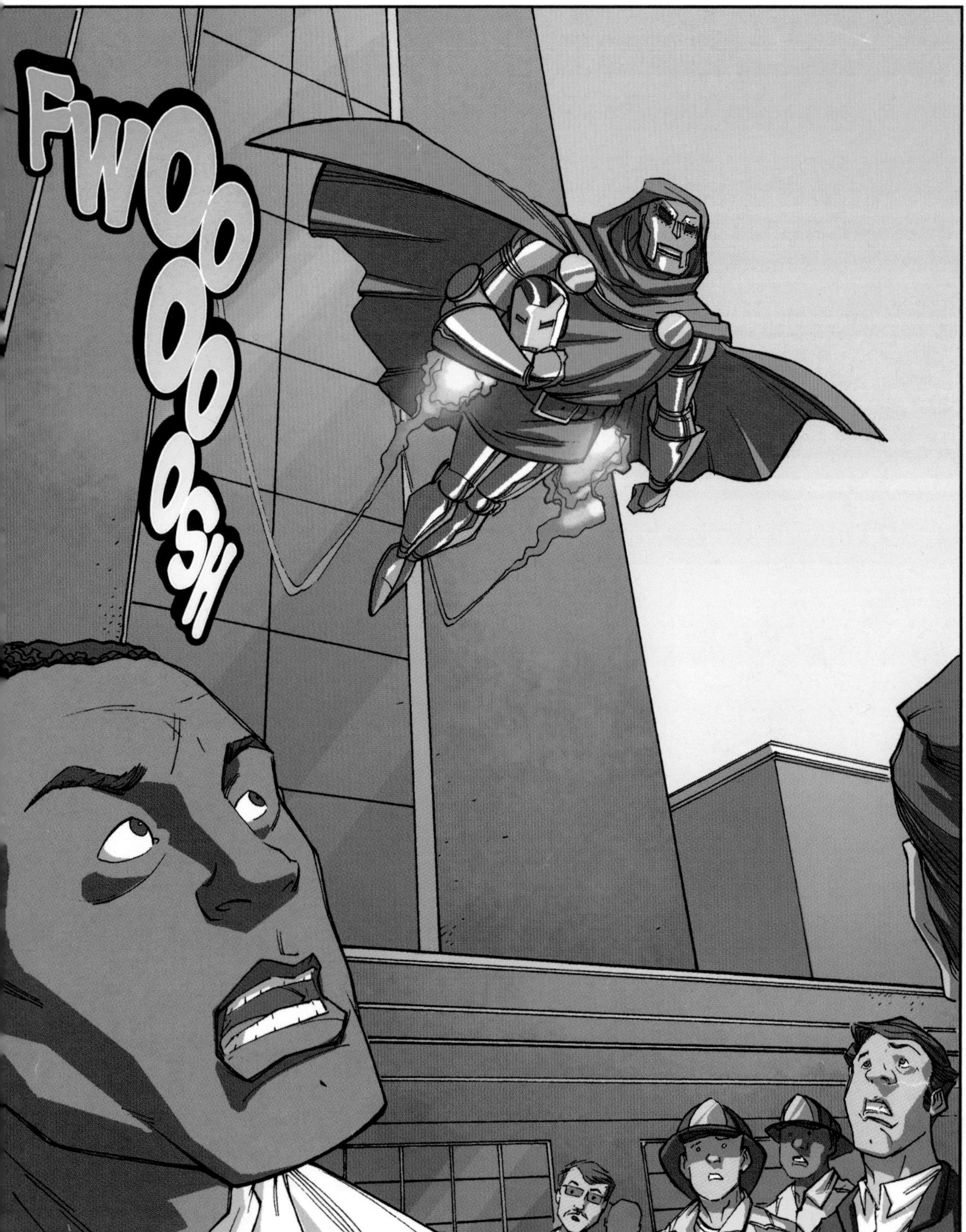
FWOOOOOOSH

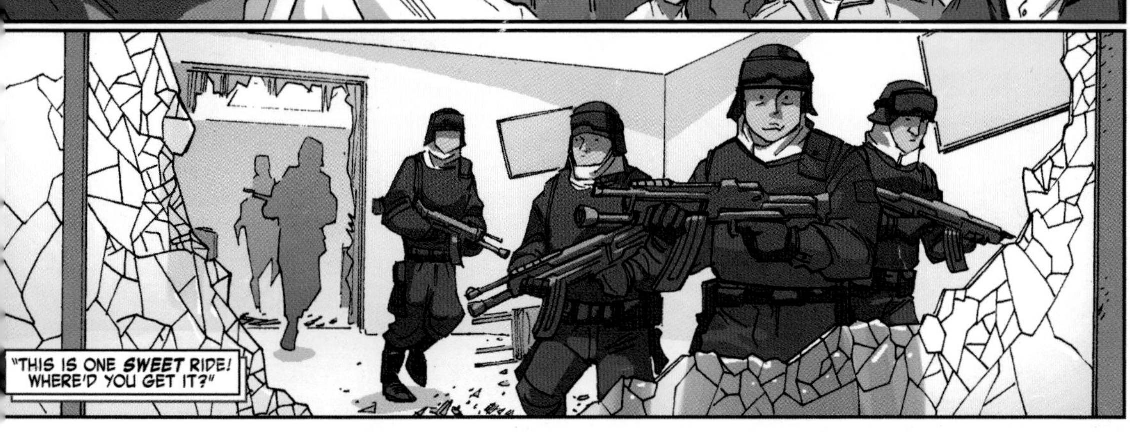
"THIS IS ONE SWEET RIDE! WHERE'D YOU GET IT?"

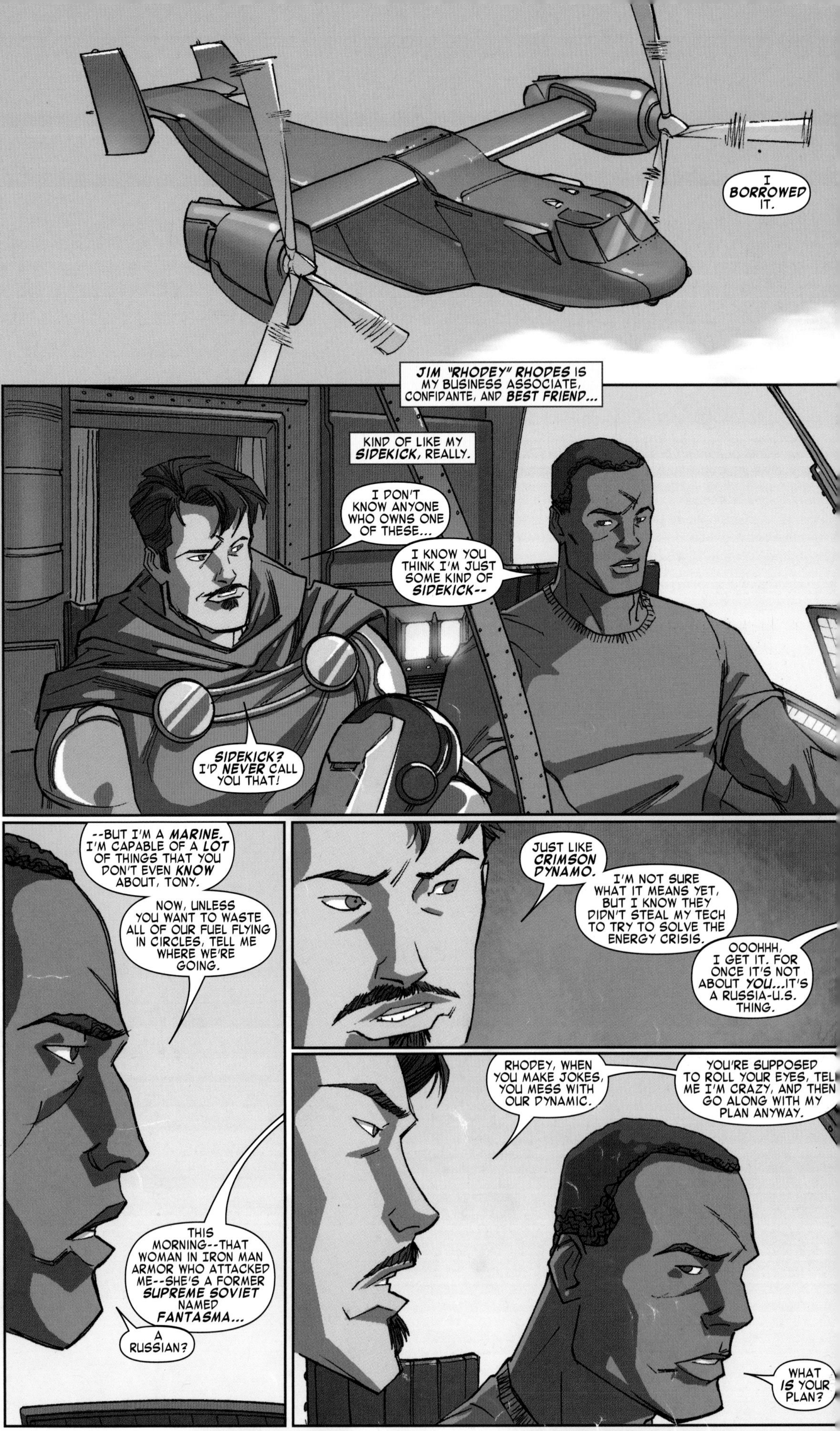
I BORROWED IT.
JIM "RHODEY" RHODES IS MY BUSINESS ASSOCIATE, CONFIDANTE, AND BEST FRIEND...
KIND OF LIKE MY SIDEKICK, REALLY.
I DON'T KNOW ANYONE WHO OWNS ONE OF THESE...
I KNOW YOU THINK I'M JUST SOME KIND OF SIDEKICK--
SIDEKICK? I'D NEVER CALL YOU THAT!
--BUT I'M A MARINE. I'M CAPABLE OF A LOT OF THINGS THAT YOU DON'T EVEN KNOW ABOUT, TONY.
NOW, UNLESS YOU WANT TO WASTE ALL OF OUR FUEL FLYING IN CIRCLES, TELL ME WHERE WE'RE GOING.
THIS MORNING--THAT WOMAN IN IRON MAN ARMOR WHO ATTACKED ME--SHE'S A FORMER SUPREME SOVIET NAMED FANTASMA...
A RUSSIAN?
JUST LIKE CRIMSON DYNAMO.
I'M NOT SURE WHAT IT MEANS YET, BUT I KNOW THEY DIDN'T STEAL MY TECH TO TRY TO SOLVE THE ENERGY CRISIS.
OOOHHH, I GET IT. FOR ONCE IT'S NOT ABOUT YOU...IT'S A RUSSIA-U.S. THING.
RHODEY, WHEN YOU MAKE JOKES, YOU MESS WITH OUR DYNAMIC.
YOU'RE SUPPOSED TO ROLL YOUR EYES, TELL ME I'M CRAZY, AND THEN GO ALONG WITH MY PLAN ANYWAY.
WHAT IS YOUR PLAN?

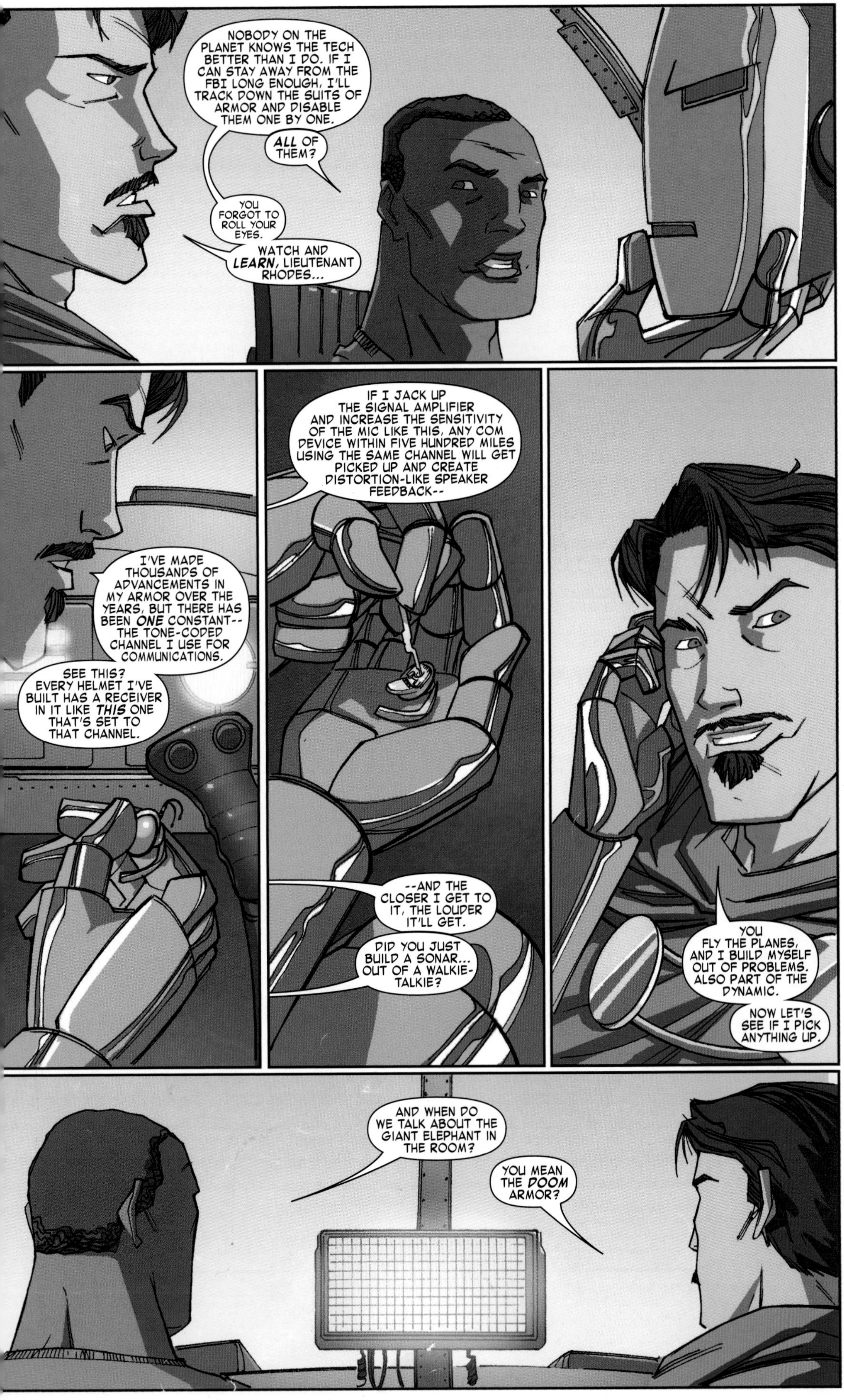
NOBODY ON THE PLANET KNOWS THE TECH BETTER THAN I DO. IF I CAN STAY AWAY FROM THE FBI LONG ENOUGH, I'LL TRACK DOWN THE SUITS OF ARMOR AND DISABLE THEM ONE BY ONE.
ALL OF THEM?
YOU FORGOT TO ROLL YOUR EYES.
WATCH AND LEARN, LIEUTENANT RHODES...
I'VE MADE THOUSANDS OF ADVANCEMENTS IN MY ARMOR OVER THE YEARS, BUT THERE HAS BEEN ONE CONSTANT-- THE TONE-CODED CHANNEL I USE FOR COMMUNICATIONS.
SEE THIS? EVERY HELMET I'VE BUILT HAS A RECEIVER IN IT LIKE THIS ONE THAT'S SET TO THAT CHANNEL.
IF I JACK UP THE SIGNAL AMPLIFIER AND INCREASE THE SENSITIVITY OF THE MIC LIKE THIS, ANY COM DEVICE WITHIN FIVE HUNDRED MILES USING THE SAME CHANNEL WILL GET PICKED UP AND CREATE DISTORTION-LIKE SPEAKER FEEDBACK--
--AND THE CLOSER I GET TO IT, THE LOUDER IT'LL GET.
DID YOU JUST BUILD A SONAR... OUT OF A WALKIE-TALKIE?
YOU FLY THE PLANES, AND I BUILD MYSELF OUT OF PROBLEMS. ALSO PART OF THE DYNAMIC.
NOW LET'S SEE IF I PICK ANYTHING UP.
AND WHEN DO WE TALK ABOUT THE GIANT ELEPHANT IN THE ROOM?
YOU MEAN THE DOOM ARMOR?

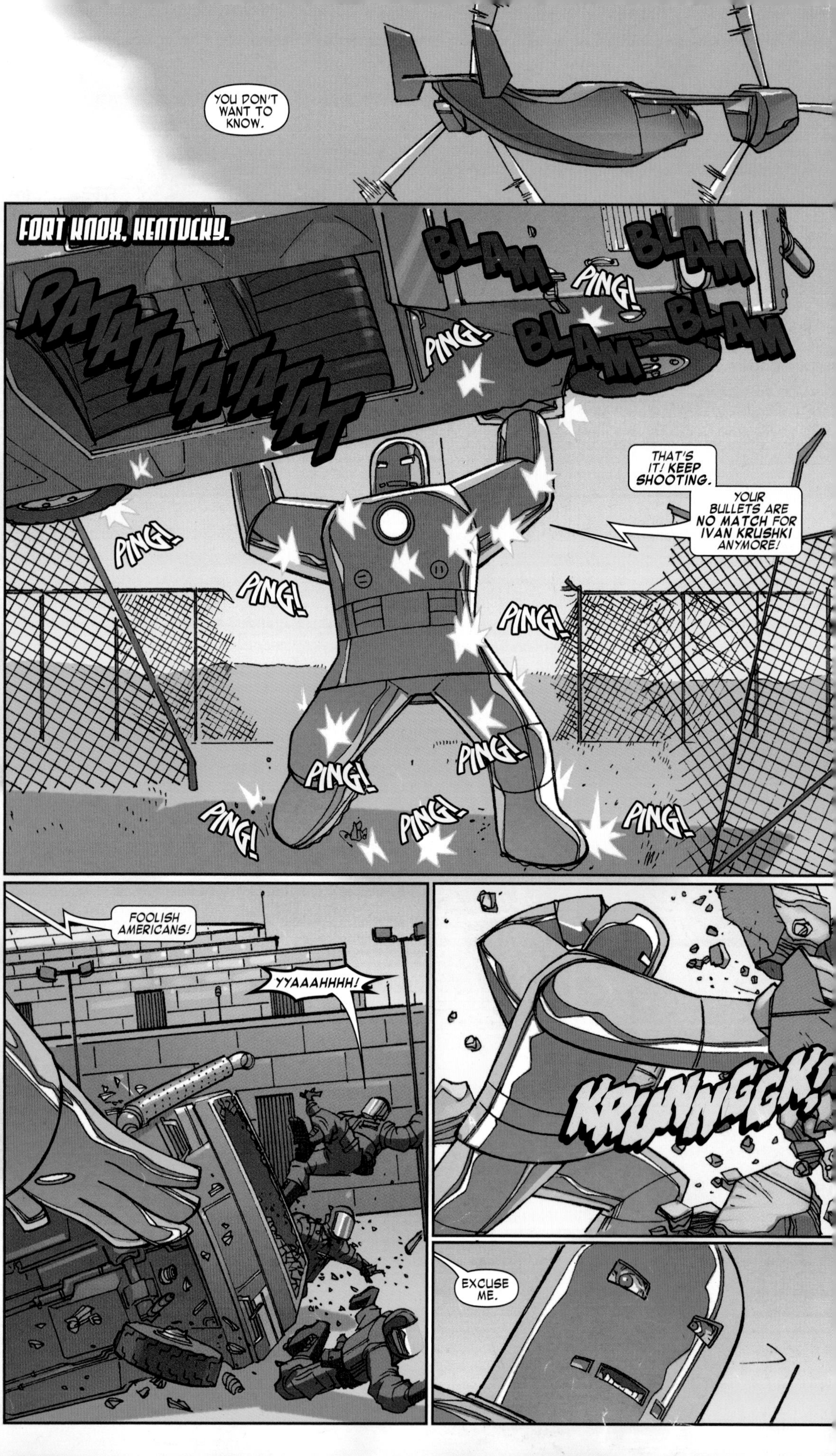
YOU DON'T WANT TO KNOW.
FORT KNOX, KENTUCKY.
RATATATATATATAT
BLAM
BLAM
PING!
BLAM
BLAM
PING!
THAT'S IT! KEEP SHOOTING.
YOUR BULLETS ARE NO MATCH FOR IVAN KRUSHKI ANYMORE!
PING!
PING!
PING!
PING!
PING!
PING!
PING!
PING!
FOOLISH AMERICANS!
YYAAAHHHH!
KRUNNGK!
EXCUSE ME.

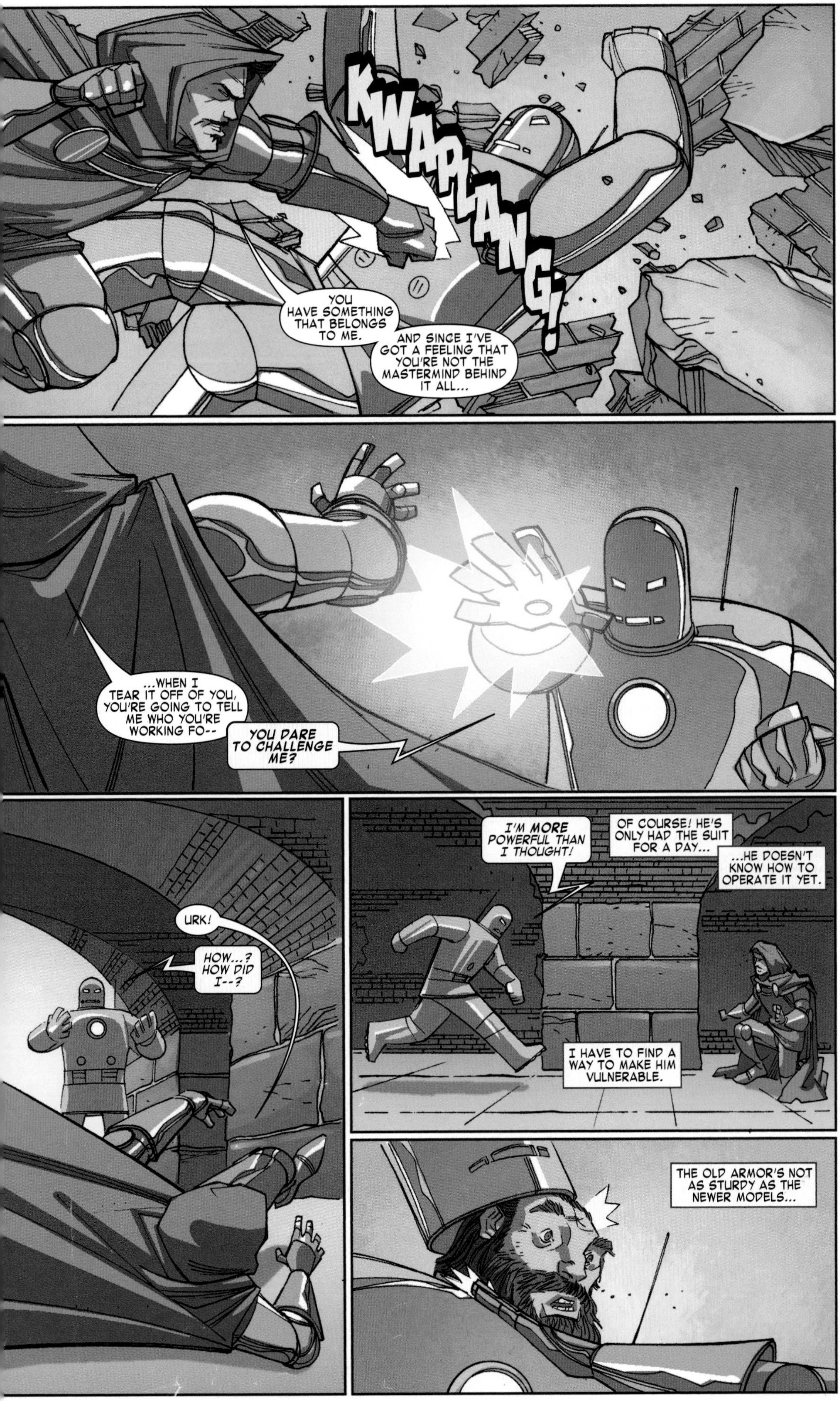
KWAPLANG!
YOU HAVE SOMETHING THAT BELONGS TO ME.
AND SINCE I'VE GOT A FEELING THAT YOU'RE NOT THE MASTERMIND BEHIND IT ALL...
...WHEN I TEAR IT OFF OF YOU, YOU'RE GOING TO TELL ME WHO YOU'RE WORKING FO--
YOU DARE TO CHALLENGE ME?
URK!
HOW...? HOW DID I--?
I'M MORE POWERFUL THAN I THOUGHT!
OF COURSE! HE'S ONLY HAD THE SUIT FOR A DAY...
...HE DOESN'T KNOW HOW TO OPERATE IT YET.
I HAVE TO FIND A WAY TO MAKE HIM VULNERABLE.
THE OLD ARMOR'S NOT AS STURDY AS THE NEWER MODELS...

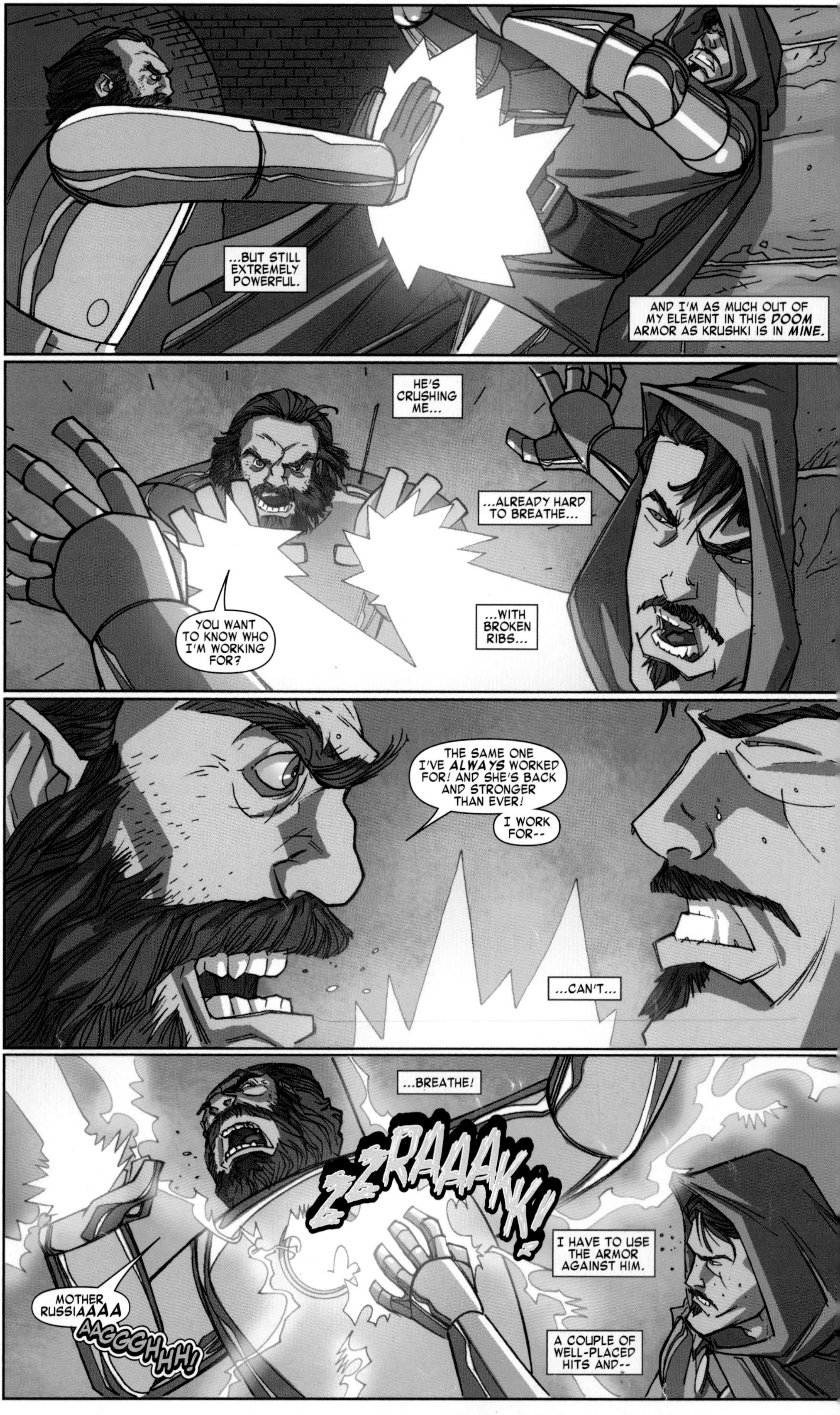
...BUT STILL EXTREMELY POWERFUL.
AND I'M AS MUCH OUT OF MY ELEMENT IN THIS DOOM ARMOR AS KRUSHKI IS IN MINE.
HE'S CRUSHING ME...
...ALREADY HARD TO BREATHE...
...WITH BROKEN RIBS...
YOU WANT TO KNOW WHO I'M WORKING FOR?
THE SAME ONE I'VE ALWAYS WORKED FOR! AND SHE'S BACK AND STRONGER THAN EVER!
I WORK FOR--
...CAN'T...
...BREATHE!
ZZRAAAKK!
I HAVE TO USE THE ARMOR AGAINST HIM.
MOTHER RUSSIAAAA
AAGGGHHH!
A COUPLE OF WELL-PLACED HITS AND--

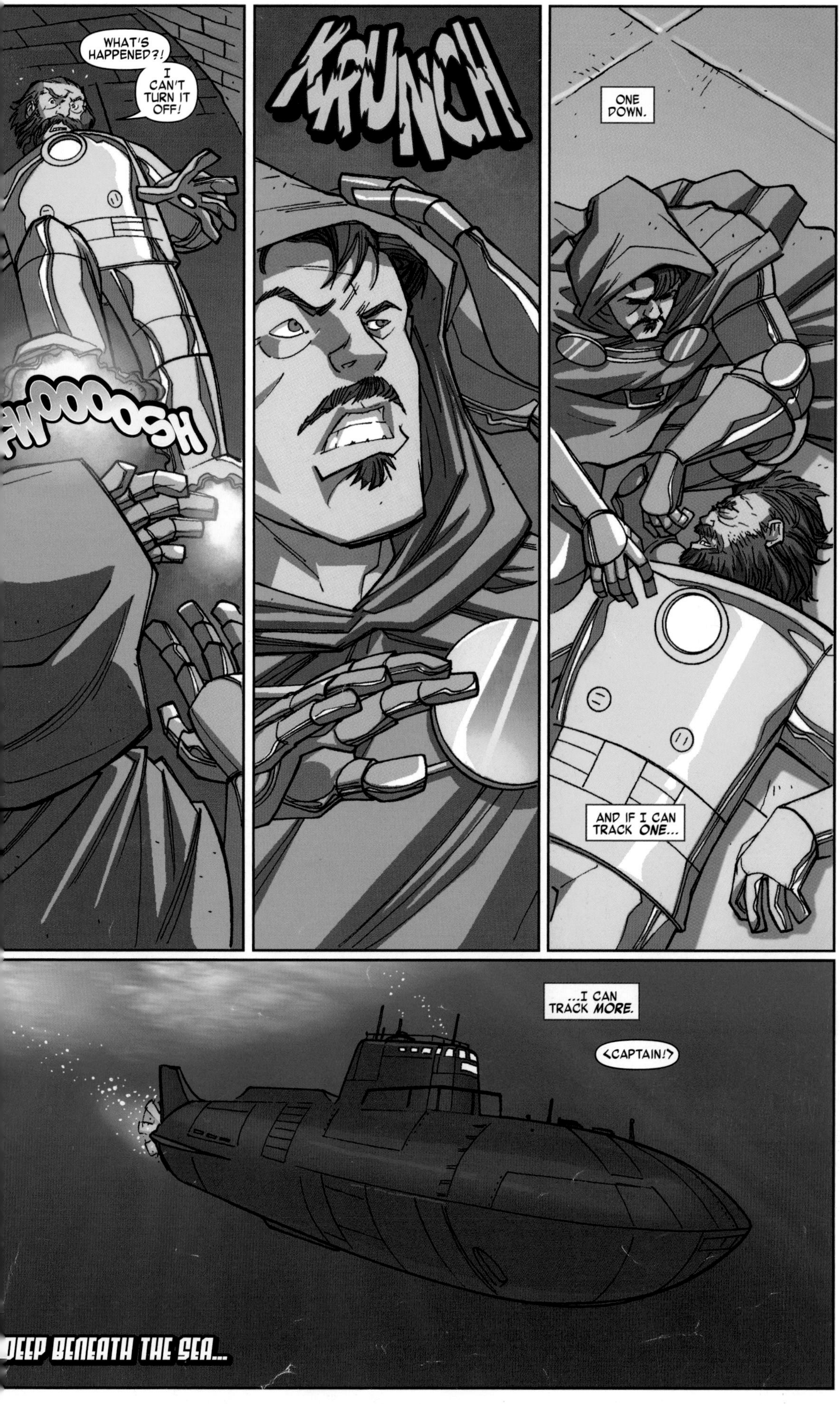
WHAT'S HAPPENED?!
I CAN'T TURN IT OFF!
FWOOOOOSH
KRUNCH
ONE DOWN.
AND IF I CAN TRACK ONE...
...I CAN TRACK MORE.
<CAPTAIN!>
DEEP BENEATH THE SEA...

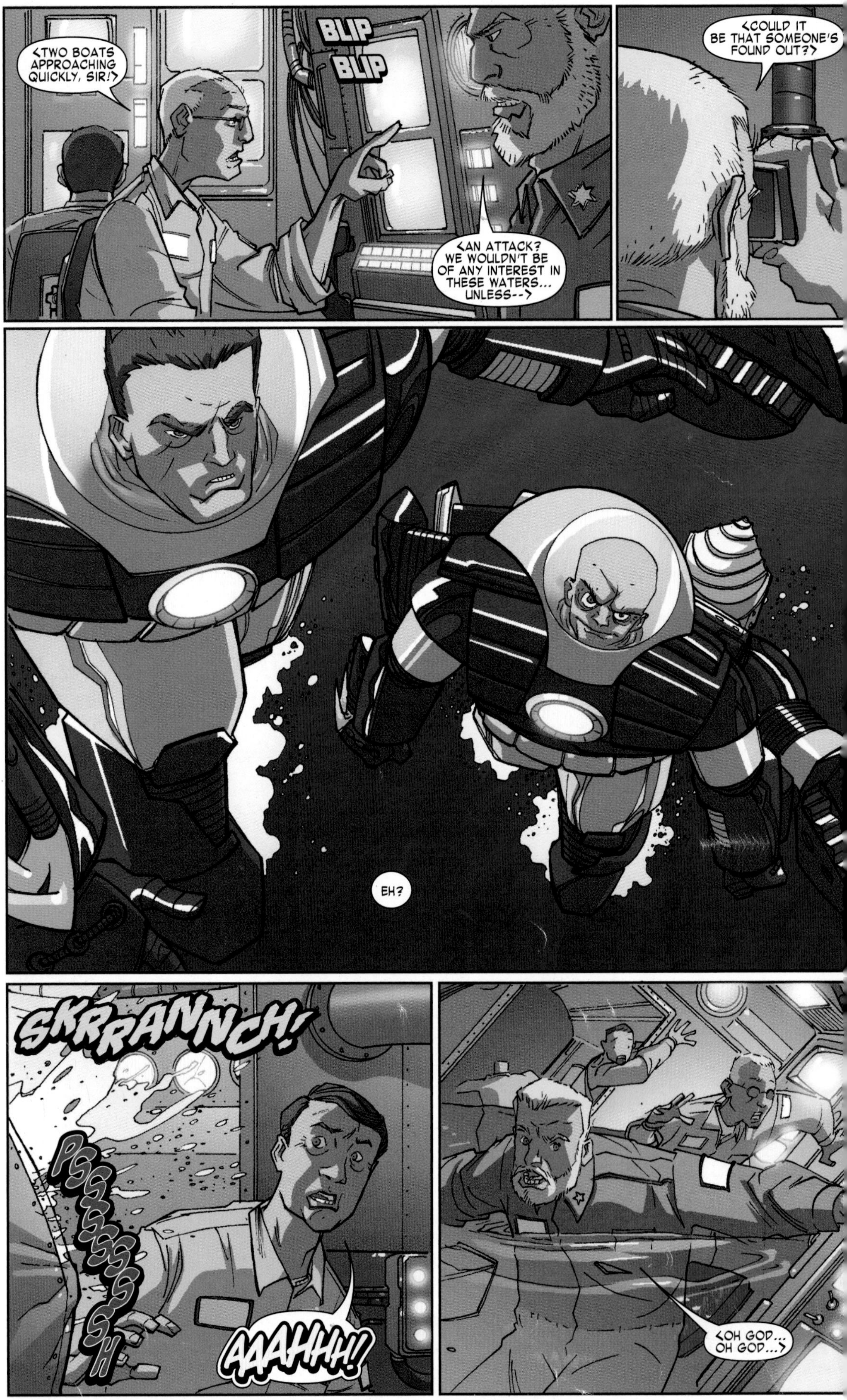

<TWO BOATS APPROACHING QUICKLY, SIR!>
BLIP
BLIP
<AN ATTACK? WE WOULDN'T BE OF ANY INTEREST IN THESE WATERS... UNLESS-->
<COULD IT BE THAT SOMEONE'S FOUND OUT?>
EH?
SKRRANNCH!
PSSSSSSSH
AAAHHH!
<OH GOD... OH GOD...>

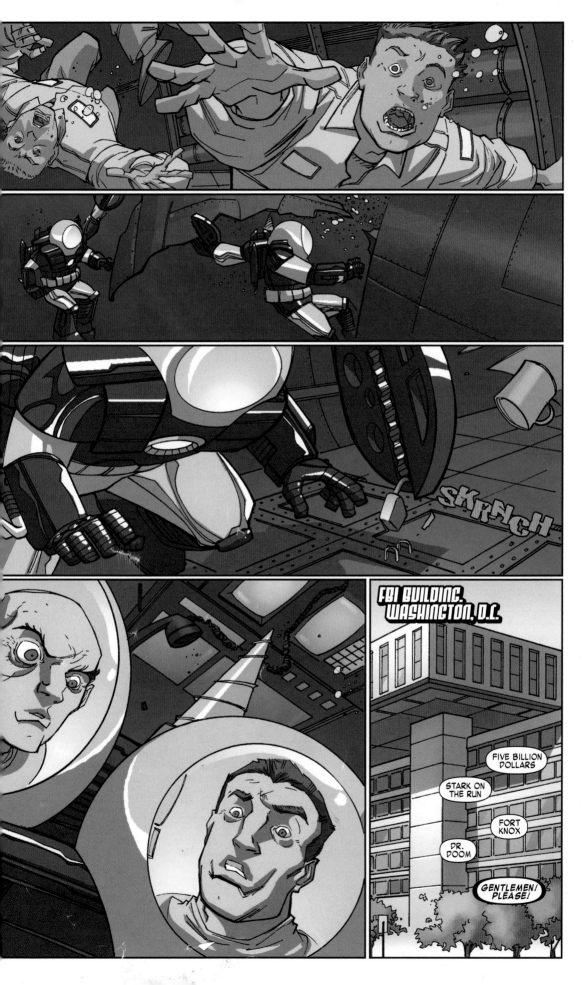

SKRNCH

FBI BUILDING. WASHINGTON, D.C.

FIVE BILLION DOLLARS

STARK ON THE RUN

FORT KNOX

DR. DOOM

GENTLEMEN! PLEASE!

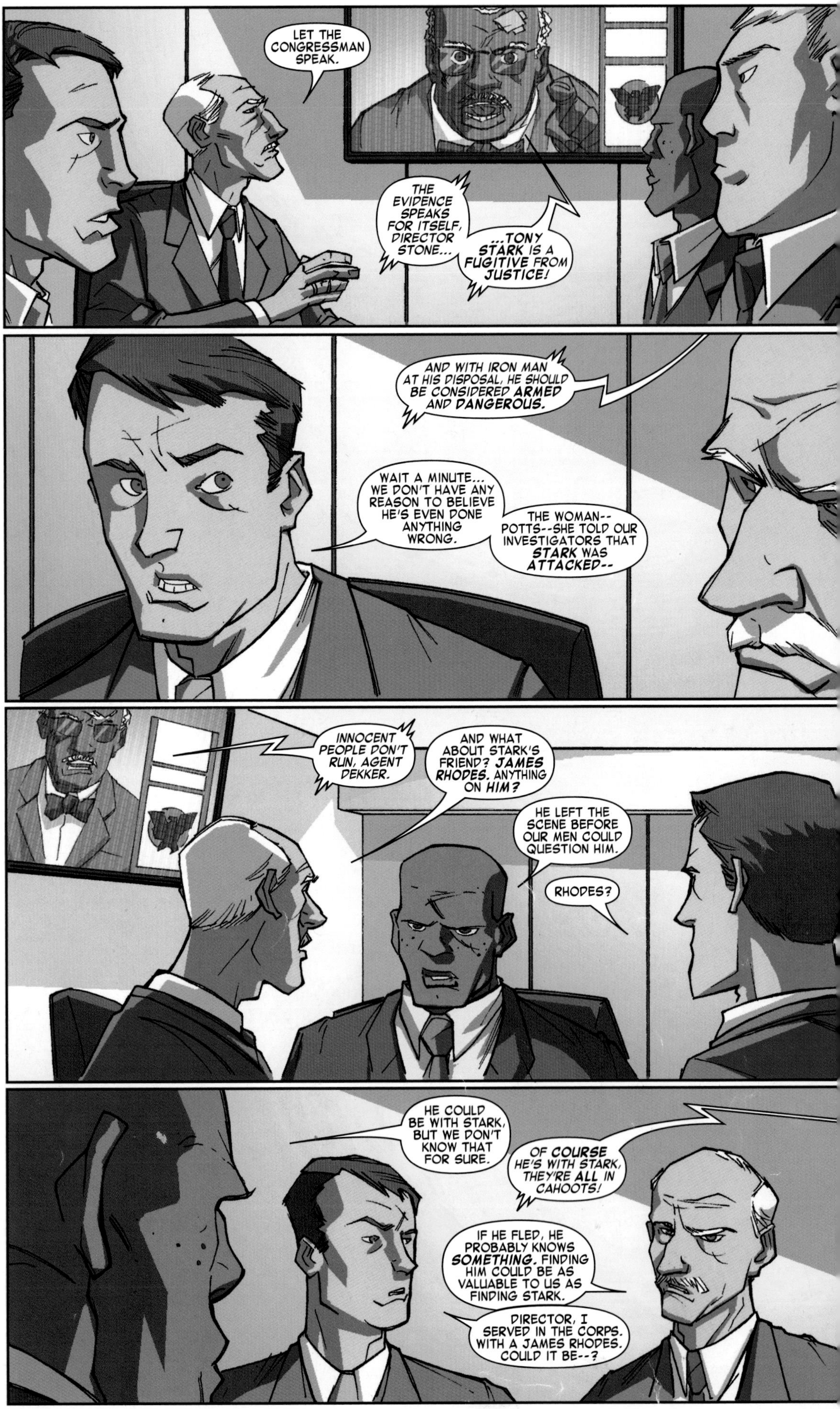
LET THE CONGRESSMAN SPEAK.
THE EVIDENCE SPEAKS FOR ITSELF, DIRECTOR STONE...
...TONY STARK IS A FUGITIVE FROM JUSTICE!
AND WITH IRON MAN AT HIS DISPOSAL, HE SHOULD BE CONSIDERED ARMED AND DANGEROUS.
WAIT A MINUTE... WE DON'T HAVE ANY REASON TO BELIEVE HE'S EVEN DONE ANYTHING WRONG.
THE WOMAN-- POTTS--SHE TOLD OUR INVESTIGATORS THAT STARK WAS ATTACKED--
INNOCENT PEOPLE DON'T RUN, AGENT DEKKER.
AND WHAT ABOUT STARK'S FRIEND? JAMES RHODES. ANYTHING ON HIM?
HE LEFT THE SCENE BEFORE OUR MEN COULD QUESTION HIM.
RHODES?
HE COULD BE WITH STARK, BUT WE DON'T KNOW THAT FOR SURE.
OF COURSE HE'S WITH STARK, THEY'RE ALL IN CAHOOTS!
IF HE FLED, HE PROBABLY KNOWS SOMETHING. FINDING HIM COULD BE AS VALUABLE TO US AS FINDING STARK.
DIRECTOR, I SERVED IN THE CORPS. WITH A JAMES RHODES. COULD IT BE--?

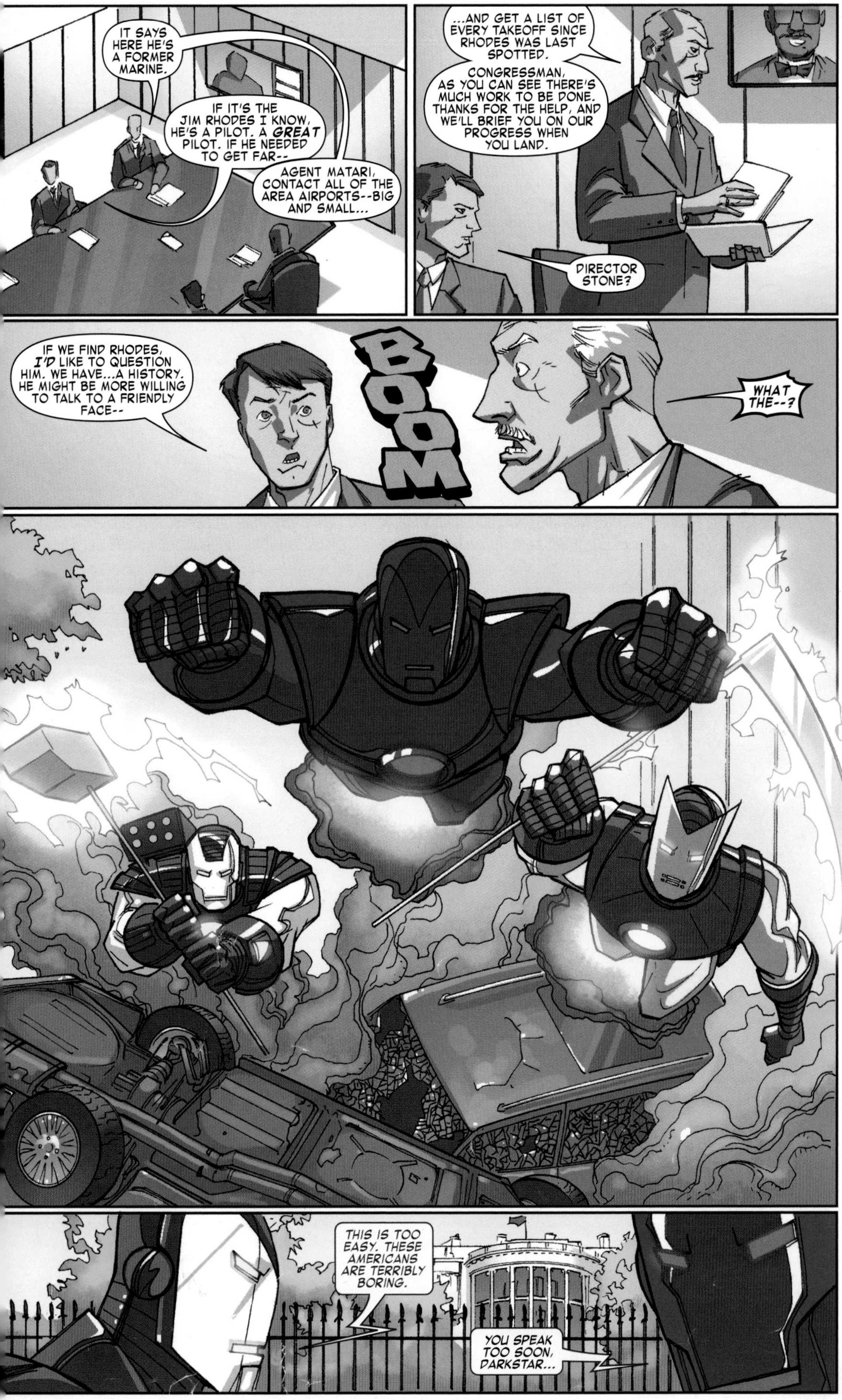
IT SAYS HERE HE'S A FORMER MARINE.
IF IT'S THE JIM RHODES I KNOW, HE'S A PILOT. A GREAT PILOT. IF HE NEEDED TO GET FAR--
AGENT MATARI, CONTACT ALL OF THE AREA AIRPORTS--BIG AND SMALL...
...AND GET A LIST OF EVERY TAKEOFF SINCE RHODES WAS LAST SPOTTED.
CONGRESSMAN, AS YOU CAN SEE THERE'S MUCH WORK TO BE DONE. THANKS FOR THE HELP, AND WE'LL BRIEF YOU ON OUR PROGRESS WHEN YOU LAND.
DIRECTOR STONE?
IF WE FIND RHODES, I'D LIKE TO QUESTION HIM. WE HAVE...A HISTORY. HE MIGHT BE MORE WILLING TO TALK TO A FRIENDLY FACE--
BOOM
WHAT THE--?
THIS IS TOO EASY. THESE AMERICANS ARE TERRIBLY BORING.
YOU SPEAK TOO SOON, DARKSTAR...

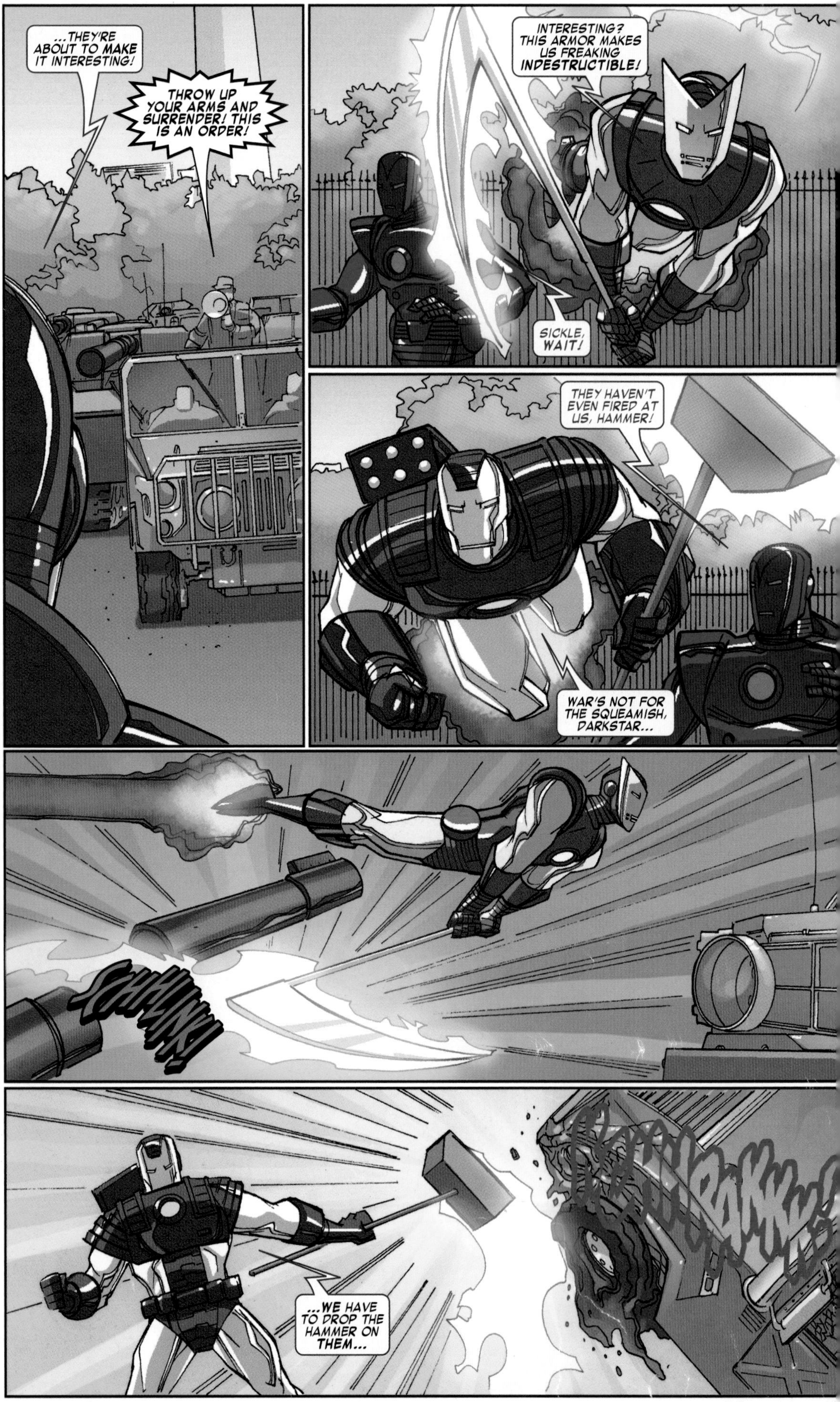
...THEY'RE ABOUT TO MAKE IT INTERESTING!
THROW UP YOUR ARMS AND SURRENDER! THIS IS AN ORDER!
INTERESTING? THIS ARMOR MAKES US FREAKING INDESTRUCTIBLE!
SICKLE, WAIT!
THEY HAVEN'T EVEN FIRED AT US, HAMMER!
WAR'S NOT FOR THE SQUEAMISH, DARKSTAR...
SCHWANK!
...WE HAVE TO DROP THE HAMMER ON THEM...

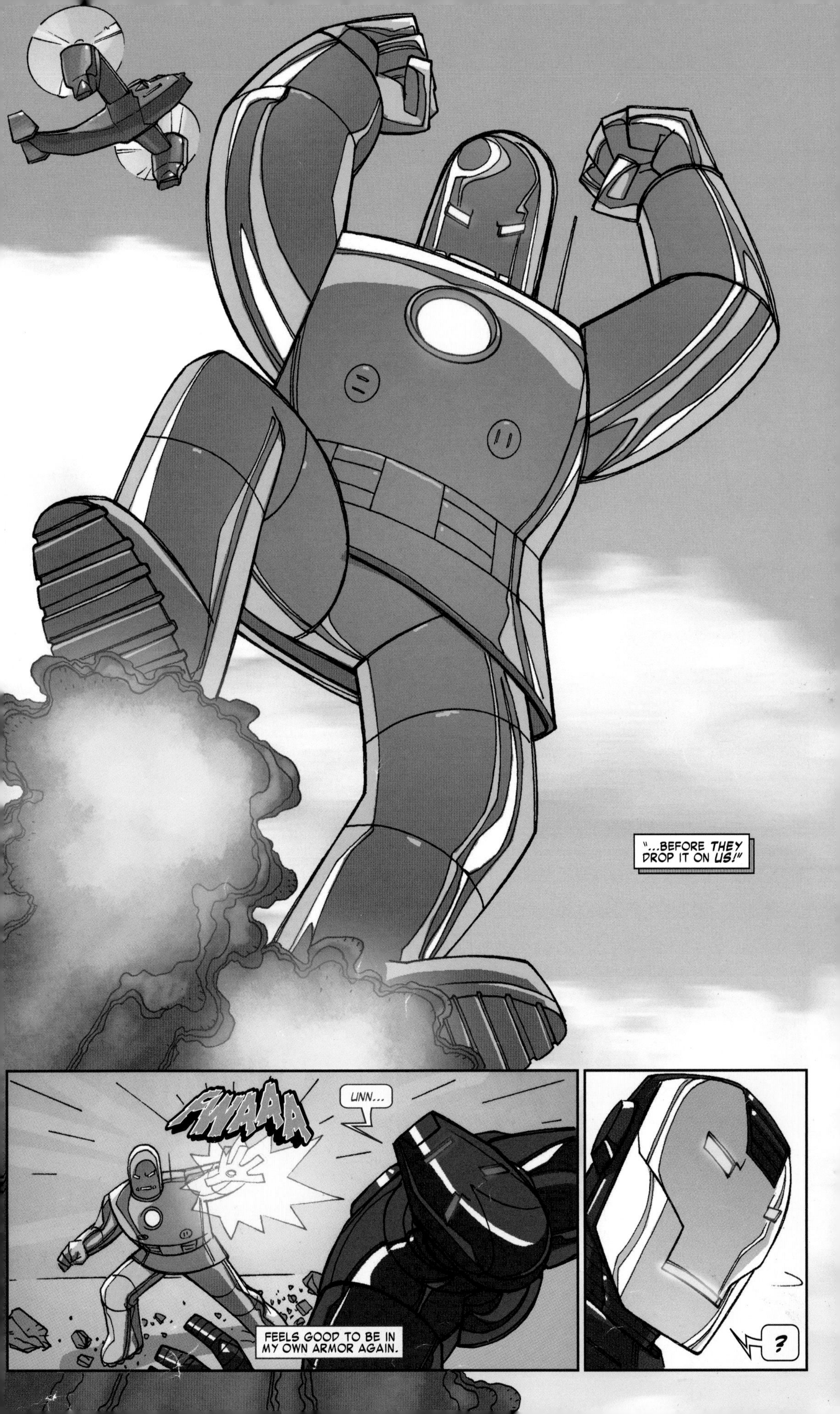
"...BEFORE THEY DROP IT ON US!"
FWAAA
UNN...
FEELS GOOD TO BE IN MY OWN ARMOR AGAIN.
?

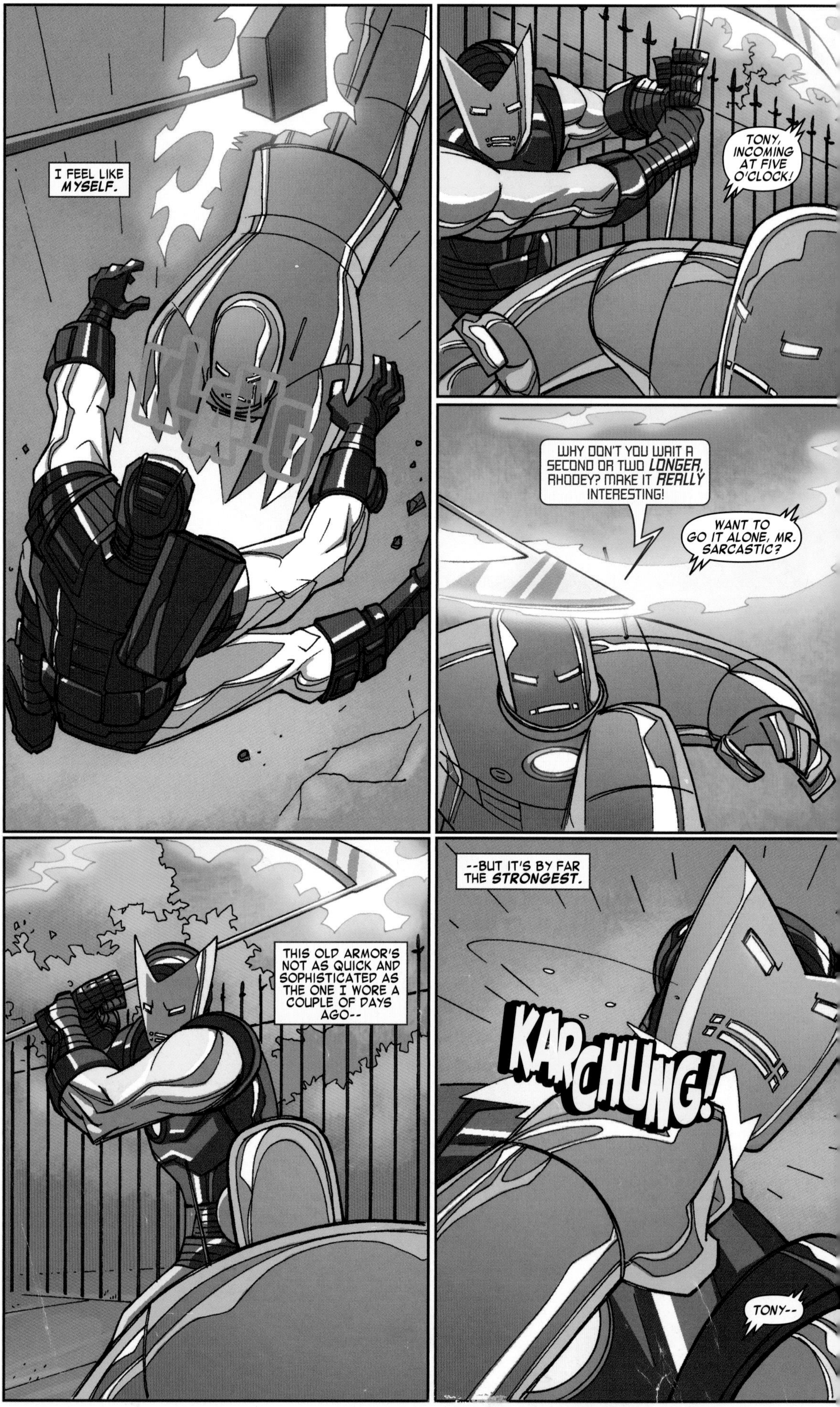
I FEEL LIKE MYSELF.
TONY, INCOMING AT FIVE O'CLOCK!
WHY DON'T YOU WAIT A SECOND OR TWO LONGER, RHODEY? MAKE IT REALLY INTERESTING!
WANT TO GO IT ALONE, MR. SARCASTIC?
THIS OLD ARMOR'S NOT AS QUICK AND SOPHISTICATED AS THE ONE I WORE A COUPLE OF DAYS AGO--
--BUT IT'S BY FAR THE STRONGEST.
KARCHUNG!
TONY--

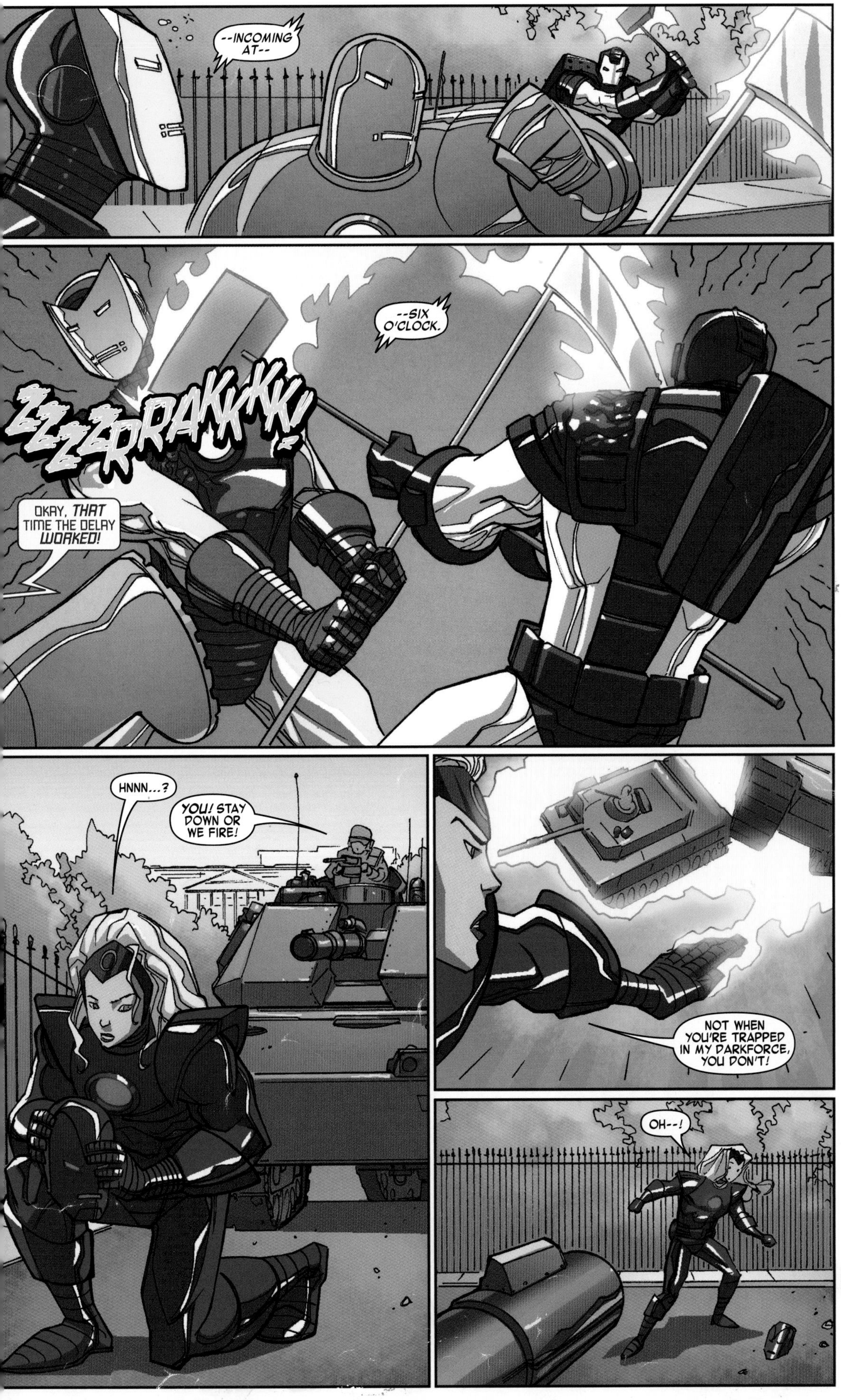
--INCOMING AT--
--SIX O'CLOCK.
ZZZZRRAKKKK!
OKAY, THAT TIME THE DELAY WORKED!
HNNN...?
YOU! STAY DOWN OR WE FIRE!
NOT WHEN YOU'RE TRAPPED IN MY DARKFORCE, YOU DON'T!
OH--!

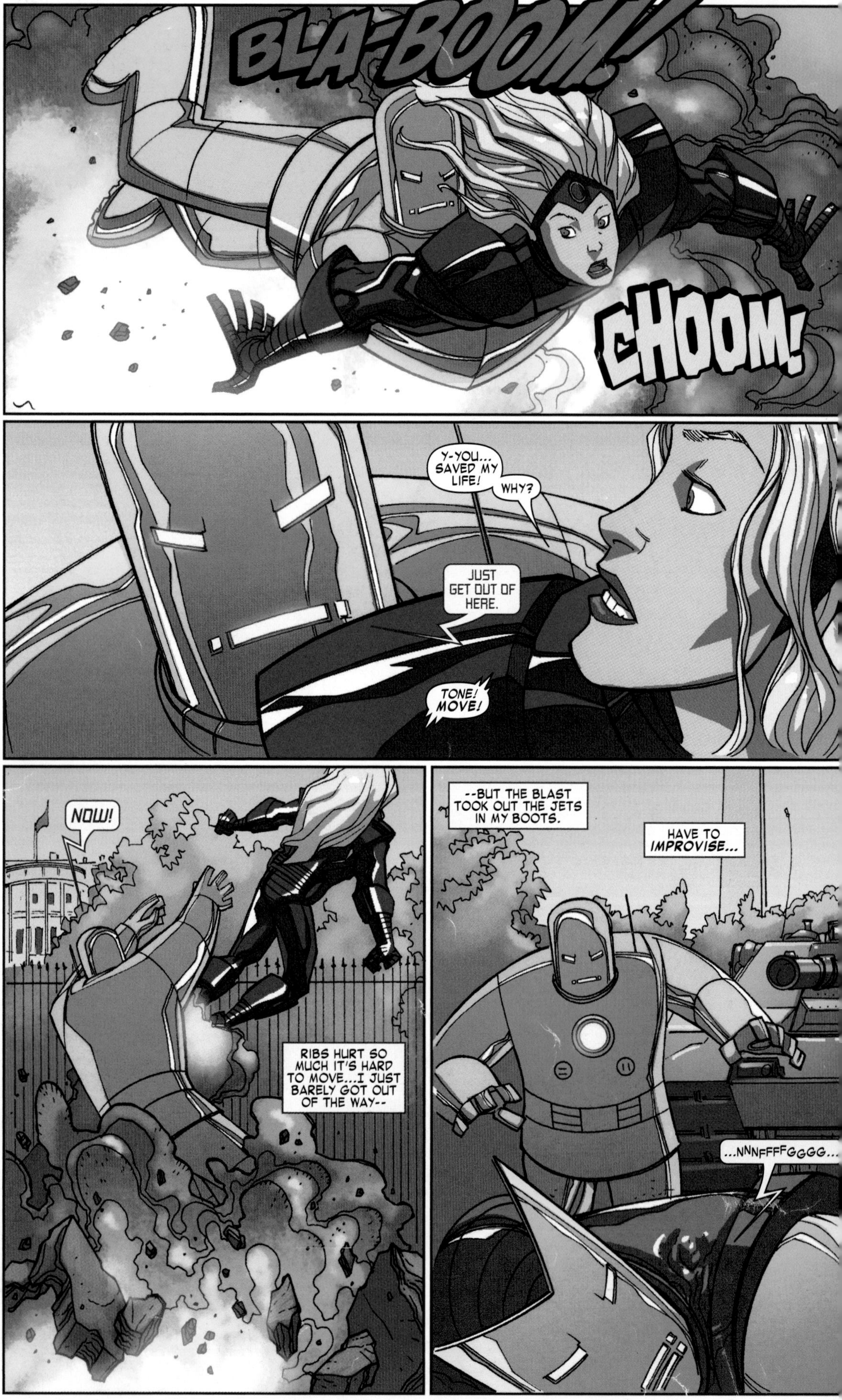
BLA-BOOM!
CHOOM!
Y-YOU... SAVED MY LIFE!
WHY?
JUST GET OUT OF HERE.
TONE! MOVE!
NOW!
RIBS HURT SO MUCH IT'S HARD TO MOVE...I JUST BARELY GOT OUT OF THE WAY--
--BUT THE BLAST TOOK OUT THE JETS IN MY BOOTS.
HAVE TO IMPROVISE...
...NNNFFFFGGGG...

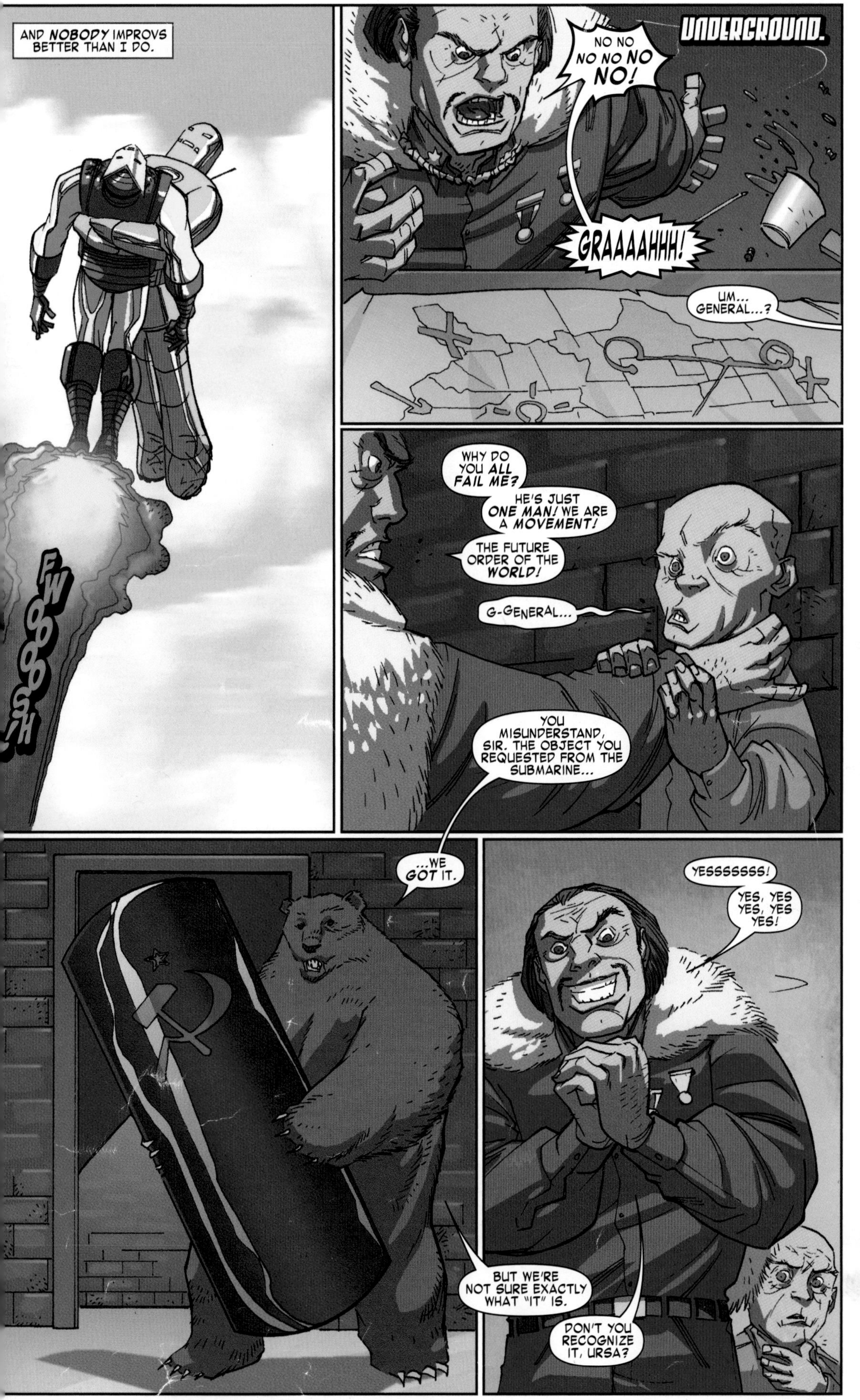

AND NOBODY IMPROVS BETTER THAN I DO.
FWOOOOSH
UNDERGROUND.
NO NO NO NO NO NO!
GRAAAAHHH!
UM... GENERAL...?
WHY DO YOU ALL FAIL ME?
HE'S JUST ONE MAN! WE ARE A MOVEMENT!
THE FUTURE ORDER OF THE WORLD!
G-GENERAL...
YOU MISUNDERSTAND, SIR. THE OBJECT YOU REQUESTED FROM THE SUBMARINE...
...WE GOT IT.
YESSSSSSS!
YES, YES YES, YES YES!
BUT WE'RE NOT SURE EXACTLY WHAT "IT" IS.
DON'T YOU RECOGNIZE IT, URSA?

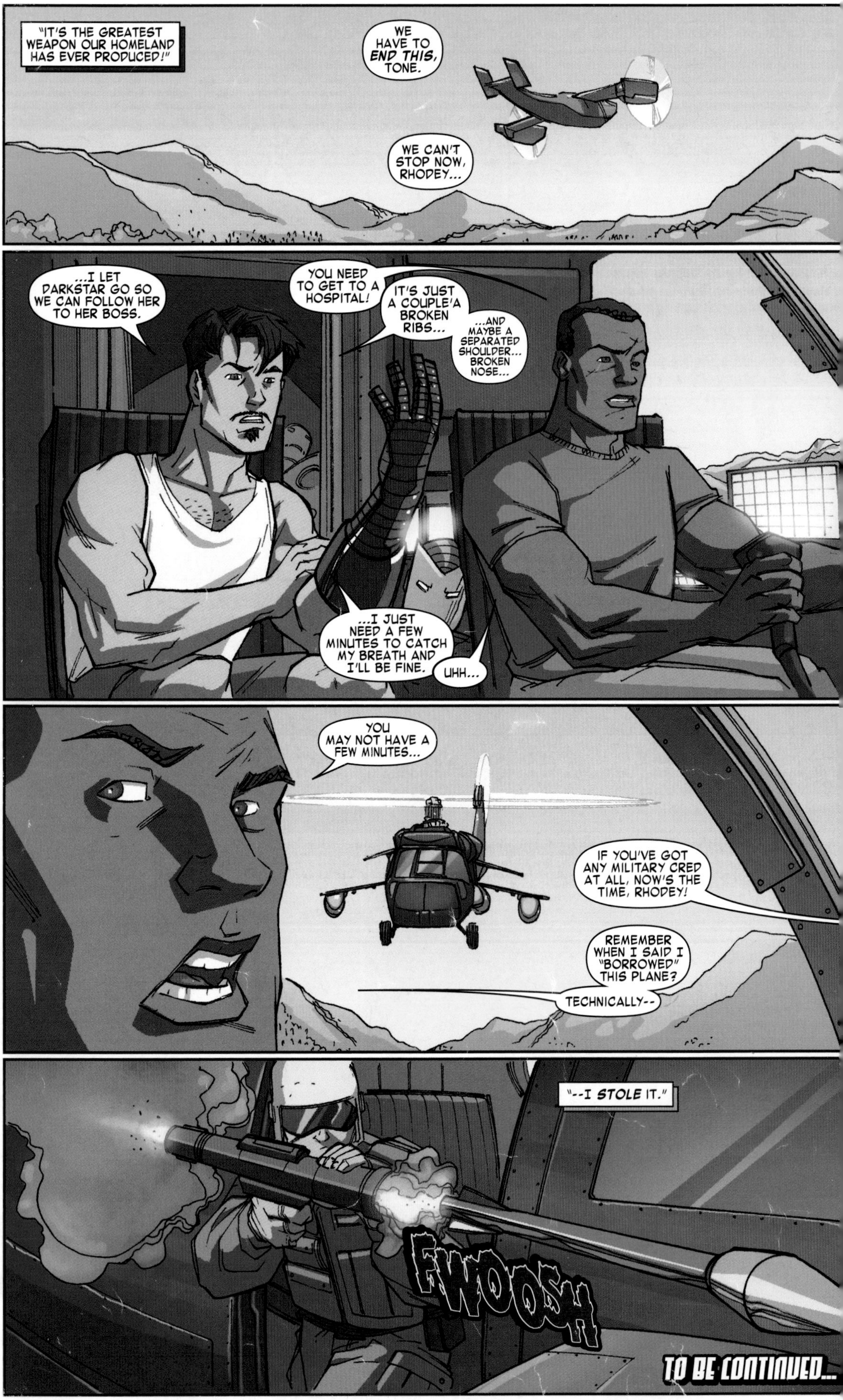
"IT'S THE GREATEST WEAPON OUR HOMELAND HAS EVER PRODUCED!"
WE HAVE TO END THIS, TONE.
WE CAN'T STOP NOW, RHODEY...
...I LET DARKSTAR GO SO WE CAN FOLLOW HER TO HER BOSS.
YOU NEED TO GET TO A HOSPITAL!
IT'S JUST A COUPLE'A BROKEN RIBS...
...AND MAYBE A SEPARATED SHOULDER... BROKEN NOSE...
...I JUST NEED A FEW MINUTES TO CATCH MY BREATH AND I'LL BE FINE.
UHH...
YOU MAY NOT HAVE A FEW MINUTES...
IF YOU'VE GOT ANY MILITARY CRED AT ALL, NOW'S THE TIME, RHODEY!
REMEMBER WHEN I SAID I "BORROWED" THIS PLANE?
TECHNICALLY--
"--I STOLE IT."
FWOOSH
TO BE CONTINUED...